W9-BAR-133

You Are Special, Little One

NANCY TAFURI

Scholastic Press • *New York*

Copyright © 2003 by Nancy Tafuri

All rights reserved. Published by Scholastic Press,

a division of Scholastic Inc., PUBLISHERS SINCE 1920.

SCHOLASTIC, SCHOLASTIC PRESS, and associated logos are trademarks and/or registered trademarks of Scholastic Inc.

No part of this publication may be reproduced, or stored in a retrieval system, or transmitted in any form or by any means,

electronic, mechanical, photocopying, recording, or otherwise, without written permission of the publisher.

For information regarding permission, write to Scholastic Inc.,

Attention: Permissions Department, 557 Broadway, New York, NY 10012.

LIBRARY OF CONGRESS CATALOGING-IN-PUBLICATION DATA AVAILABLE

ISBN 0-439-39879-7

The artwork was created with watercolor inks and colored pencils.

The text is set in 22-point Iowan Bold Italic.

10   9   8   7   6   5   4   3   2   1   03   04   05   06   07

FIRST EDITION, SEPTEMBER 2003

Printed in Mexico   49

The animals featured in this book include: lion and weaver bird; agama lizard;

black-tailed prairie dog and prairie chicken; Camas pocket gopher;

king penguin and arctic tern; crabeater seal; beaver, carp, and pickerel frog; dragonfly;

eastern meadowlark and New England cottontail; bumblebee; red fox and bobwhite quail;

raccoon; and brown trout and common yellowthroat.

To Cristina
and every child . . .
you are so special.

On a hot savannah
under a shady tree,
a lion cub asks,
"How am I special?"

And Mama and Papa Lion reply,
"Dear little one,
with your dense, golden coat
and your deep, resounding purr,
you are so special,
and we will love you
forever and ever and always."

In a burrow opening
on a grassy plain,
a prairie dog pup asks,
"How am I special?"

And Mama and Papa Prairie Dog reply,
"Dear little one,
with your keen, watchful eyes
and your powerful legs for digging,
you are so special,
and we will love you
forever and ever and always."

Atop an icy floe
on a snow-fringed sea,
a penguin chick asks,
"How am I special?"

And Mama and Papa Penguin reply,
"Dear little one,
with your soft, downy coat
and your swift, graceful swimming,
you are so special,
and we will love you
forever and ever and always."

High on their lodge
in a cool, clear pond,
a beaver kit asks,
"How am I special?"

And Mama and Papa Beaver reply,
"Dear little one,
with your sleek, heavy fur
and your large, webbed feet for diving,
you are so special,
and we will love you
forever and ever and always."

Nestled in a thicket
by a farmland meadow,
a lark youngling asks,
"How am I special?"

And Mama and Papa Lark reply,
"Dear little one,
   with your bright yellow feathers
   and your light, cheerful song,
   you are so special,
   and we will love you
   forever and ever and always."

Deep in a tree trunk
by a woodland grove,
a fox cub asks,
"How am I special?"

And Mama and Papa Fox reply,
"Dear little one,
   with your red, bushy tail
   and your clever, nimble ways,
   you are so special,
   and we will love you
   forever and ever and always."

In a grassy pasture
by a gently flowing stream,
a young child asks,
"How am I special?"

And Mama and Papa reply,
"Dear little one,
 with your warm, caring heart
 and your bright, curious mind,
 you are so special,
 and we will love you
 forever and ever and always."